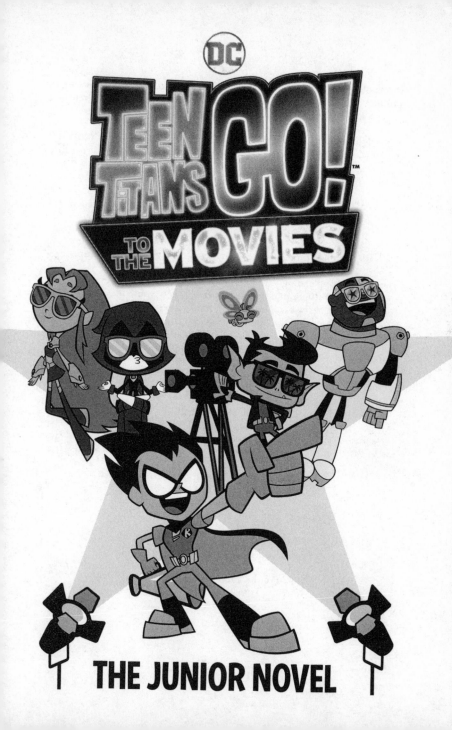

TEEN TITANS GO! TO THE MOVIES

THE JUNIOR NOVEL

Copyright © 2018 DC Comics. TEEN TITANS GO! TO THE MOVIES and all related characters and elements © & ™ DC Comics and Warner Bros. Entertainment Inc.
(s18)

Cover design by Ching Chan.

Little, Brown and Company
Hachette Book Group
1290 Avenue of the Americas, New York, NY 10104
Visit us at LBYR.com

First Edition: June 2018

Little, Brown and Company is a division of Hachette Book Group, Inc. The Little, Brown name and logo are trademarks of Hachette Book Group, Inc.

The publisher is not responsible for websites (or their content) that are not owned by the publisher.

Library of Congress Control Number 2018936314

ISBNs: 978-0-316-47598-3 (pbk.); 978-0-316-48824-2 (Scholastic ed.); 978-0-316-47601-0 (ebook)

Printed in the United States of America

LSC-C

10 9 8 7 6 5 4 3 2 1

THE JUNIOR NOVEL

Adapted by Steve Korté
Based on the screenplay by
Michael Jelenic & Aaron Horvath

Ⓛ Ⓑ

Little, Brown and Company
New York Boston

CHAPTER 1

It was a gorgeous summer afternoon in Jump City. Happy citizens were strolling down sidewalks, shopping in stores, and eating in restaurants. It was one of those perfect days when it seemed that nothing could possibly go wrong.

WHOMP! WHOMP! WHOMP!

In the distance, thunderously loud footsteps could be heard. From the sound of them, the footsteps were moving toward downtown Jump City.

THUD! THUD! THUD!

The people on the street started to panic as the noises grew louder.

Suddenly, a terrifying sight came stomping around the corner. It was a giant pink monster! The creature stood several stories tall, and it waved its puffy arms menacingly in the air. As the sun reflected off its shiny body, the citizens saw the truth: The monster was made up entirely of bright-pink balloons!

"Prepare to cower under the inflated might of Balloon Man!" the monster roared.

The crowd screamed in horror.

Balloon Man moved toward the Jump City Bank and said, "It's time to inflate my bank account!"

CRASH!

Balloon Man smashed a fist against the door of the bank and entered the building. A few minutes later, he emerged carrying the bank's safe.

The Jump City police force quickly formed a barricade of cars and police officers to block Balloon Man.

SLAM! WHAM! BAM!

The creature easily lifted its giant feet and kicked the police officers away. It looked like no one could stop Balloon Man!

Just then, the five costumed crime fighters known as the Teen Titans arrived on the scene. Robin, Raven, Starfire, Cyborg, and Beast Boy stood heroically in the middle of street. They glared at the rampaging villain.

"We's about to light this fool up!" chuckled Beast Boy. He could transform into any animal he could think of.

The alien princess warrior Starfire soared into the air and wiggled her fingers. She could fly and shoot starbolts from her eyes and hands.

"*Ooo*, I call the belly!" she said as she joyfully imagined poking her fingers into Balloon Man's pink stomach. "Pop, pop, pop, pop, pop, pop, pop, pop, pop!"

Robin, the leader of the group, took a step forward and pointed toward Balloon Man.

"Titans, *GO!*" he shouted.

"*Grrr!*" growled Balloon Man, facing the Teen Titans. "Time to play!"

With an evil chuckle, the monster transformed part of his balloon body into balloon versions of a litter of pink newborn kittens.

Starfire stopped flying toward Balloon Man. Instead, she hovered in midair and smiled with delight. She *loved* kittens.

"*Oooooh*, kitties!" she squealed, and reached out to cuddle one of the kitten balloons.

"Starfire, no!" called out Raven, who was using her demonic powers to float nearby. Because her father was a powerful demon, Raven had access to all kinds of spells.

POP!

One of the kitten balloons deflated.

"Awwww," said a disappointed Starfire. Then she reached for another kitten balloon. "Yay!"

POP!

"Awwww," she said, even more dejected, as this kitten deflated, too.

But down on the ground, Beast Boy had a plan.

POOF!

Using his superpower to change into any kind of animal he could think of, he transformed himself into a spiky green hedgehog.

"I'm gonna pop you, fool!" yelled hedgehog–Beast Boy.

ZIP! ZIP! ZIP!

Beast Boy launched a dozen hedgehog needles into the air. Direct hit! The attack poked the top of Balloon Man's round pink butt. The needles popped a huge hole on Balloon Man's right butt cheek.

BLORRRRRT!

A long and loud explosion of air blasted out of the hole.

Beast Boy rolled on the ground in laughter.

"Ha-ha!" he called out. "Big Balloon Dude farted!"

"That wasn't a fart!" said Balloon Man with a stern frown. "That was just air…leaving my butt!"

"Which is a fart," replied Raven with a smug chuckle.

The five Teen Titans started to chant.

"Balloon Man farted!" they shouted. "Balloon Man farted!"

With a sigh, Balloon Man glared at the Titans.

"You guys are *awfully* immature for the Justice League," he said.

The heroes glanced at one another with confused looks on their faces.

"Man, hold on!" said the half-man, half-robot known as Cyborg. "Do we *look* like the Justice League to you?"

"I don't know," replied Balloon Man with a shrug. "I thought maybe you were some of the lesser-known members."

The Titans frowned and stared at their opponent.

"I am the insulted!" added Starfire.

"All right, all right," said Balloon Man with a weary sigh. "Then who *are* you guys?"

Beast Boy turned to his best friend, Cyborg, and said, "Yo, Cy. This guy don't know who we is!"

"Oh, really?" replied Cyborg. "Then I think it's time we tell him!"

The Teen Titans quickly gathered together on the sidewalk. With smiles on their faces, they started singing "Teen Titans *GO!*," their insanely awesome theme song.

They had been practicing it for ages, and were really proud of it. Cyborg dropped a beat.

Beast Boy transformed himself into a tiny green cat as he sang. It was a great dramatic effect.

As Robin started his solo, the other Titans exchanged gleeful looks and quickly sang about Robin's baby hands.

Robin was self-conscious, but he really *did* have tiny hands.

As Robin sulked, Raven raised her hands to cast a magic spell for the finale:

Azarath, Metrion, Zan-zan-zan.

The Titans jumped into the air to finish their song with a rousing chant. It was a really physically taxing song and dance routine they had come up with.

Their performance was over, and as they caught their breath the Titans looked around them. Balloon Man was nowhere to be seen.

"*Aww*, yeah!" shouted Beast Boy happily. "We are *so* tough!"

"Our jams are so sick that they blew up Balloon Man!" said Robin.

Just then, the Titans noticed that three more heroes had arrived on the scene. It was the world-famous members of the Justice League: Wonder Woman, Superman, and Green Lantern.

Robin smiled at the adult super heroes and said, "Sorry, guys, but you're too late! We already took down Balloon Man!"

Wonder Woman cast an annoyed look at the Titans and then glanced down the street to see Balloon Man running away.

"Yeah, right," said Wonder Woman, rolling her eyes. "Sure you did."

Robin ignored her sarcastic remark and asked, "Since you came all this way, you guys wanna hang?"

"Yeah, well…" said Green Lantern. "You know, we would love to. But we have to get to Batman's movie premiere."

Beast Boy jumped in the air and said happily, "*Yeah!* Another Batman movie!"

"Batman is *so* cool!" added Cyborg excitedly.

Robin sighed. "It's always been my dream to have my own movie."

Superman looked down at Robin with surprise and said, "Well, it *is* important to have dreams, I guess."

"What do you mean by that?" asked Raven.

"Well…you know," said Wonder Woman hesitantly, wanting to spare Robin's feelings at least a little bit, "they only make movies about *real* heroes."

"Yeah!" agreed Green Lantern. "And Robin's just a sidekick with no superpowers…."

Robin frowned and said, "I'm *not* a sidekick anymore! I left Batman years ago and started my own super hero team!"

Green Lantern smiled condescendingly and said, "Yeah, a team that's more interested in singing songs than fighting crime?"

"You guys are"—Superman searched for just the right word—"goofsters."

"You know, with the farts?" added Wonder Woman.

"And always crackin' your jokes?" said Green Lantern.

Robin shook his head in disbelief and said, "You mean people think we're *jokes*?"

"Why do you think there's never been a movie made about you?" replied Superman.

Starfire looked up at the members of the Justice League and asked, "Well, has there been the movie about you?"

"Oh, *so* many," said Superman. "And more to come!"

"It took a while, but yes, I have my own now," replied Wonder Woman.

Superman faced the Titans and said, "The problem is that you guys are never actually doing anything *heroic*."

Cyborg looked offended and said, "Man, *please*! That ain't true! What about that time we discovered that sweet *diner*? And they had that *food*?"

The other Titans nodded their heads happily, remembering the awesomeness of the diner and its food.

"That wasn't even a *crime*!" said Superman. "You didn't save anything!"

"This guy thinks we didn't save anything," said Cyborg with disbelief. "We saved room for *dessert*!"

The other Titans were again momentarily lost in thoughts of the awesomeness of the diner's dessert.

Superman frowned and said, "Listen to me, Titans. If you keep playing the fool, only as jokes—"

Before Superman could finish his sentence, Beast Boy farted loudly.

The other Titans tried to hold it back, but they all started to giggle.

Superman sighed and turned to the other members of the Justice League.

"Anyway, we gotta get going or we'll be late for the premiere," he said.

Seconds later, the three Justice League heroes

soared into the air and disappeared over the Jump City skyline.

A worried look filled Starfire's face. She turned to the other Titans.

"Is it true?" she asked nervously. "Are we not the real heroes?"

Robin quickly replied, "Of *course* we are! We just took down Balloon Man!"

As the Titans smiled in agreement, Robin announced, "Now, I believe we have a premiere to attend! Titans, *GO*...to the movies!"

CHAPTER 2

Across town, a dozen bright spotlights were carving up the nighttime sky above Jump City. Photographers, reporters, and a large crowd of fans were gathered outside the city's largest and most glamorous movie theater. They were there to celebrate the premiere of the newest, most expensive, most amazing super hero movie ever. Reports were that it was even better than the most expensive and most amazing super hero movie that had opened in the same theater the previous week.

A swirling hologram of Batman was projected in front of the theater. A television crew was stationed nearby, and a reporter was conducting interviews with world-famous super heroes as they made their appearances on the red carpet.

Supergirl was the first to arrive. She was dressed in a glamorous full-length red gown.

"What are you wearing tonight?" the reporter asked.

Supergirl smiled and replied, "Plastic Man."

All of a sudden, Supergirl's red dress spoke to the reporter!

"Hey, John, how are you?" asked the shape-shifting hero Plastic Man. He had transformed himself into Supergirl's outfit for the evening.

Next to arrive was Wonder Woman, stylishly attired in her finest star-spangled Amazonian outfit.

Camera flashes filled the air as a crowd of photographers started shouting excitedly, "Wonder Woman! Show us that move! Show us the bracelets!"

Wonder Woman smiled obligingly and slammed her magical Amazonian bracelets together.

BLAM!

The resulting sonic blast from her bracelets rushed into the photographers and knocked them clear down the block.

Wonder Woman cheerily waved to her fans and continued into the theater.

The Teen Titans were standing across the street. They watched the proceedings with awe.

"Come on, Titans," said Robin. "This is every super hero's dream—to have your own movie!"

"Not my dream," said Raven.

"Yeah, who cares?" agreed Cyborg.

"Not I," replied Starfire.

Beast Boy held a giant burrito in his hand. He opened his mouth wide and said, "This *burrito* is my dream!" as he started chowing down.

"Fine!" said Robin with disgust. He started to cross the street. "It's *my* dream! But one day, it's going to come true! Now, Titans...are you ready to walk the red carpet?"

The other Titans shrugged and followed Robin. Just as they reached the red carpet, another super hero arrived. It was the microscopic crime fighter known as the Atom.

"The Atom has arrived!" his tiny voice announced. *WHAM!*

Robin's boot-clad foot stepped directly on top of the Atom.

Robin marched to the front of the theater. There, he paused for just a second to shake his foot and get the Atom off the bottom of his boot, where he was desperately clinging.

"Behold!" said Robin as he raised his hand dramatically and walked up to a security guard at the end of the red carpet. The guard was holding a clipboard, and he peered down at Robin and the other Titans.

The guard reached out his hand to stop them from entering the theater.

"Hold it," he said. "This premiere is for super heroes only. Who are you?"

"Who are we?" Robin said with disbelief. "Who are *we*?"

Beast Boy laughed and said, "This fool don't knows who we is!"

"Perhaps this will remind you?" offered Cyborg as he pulled out the trusty cassette tape with their background music. It was stylishly labeled "Who We Is."

The Titans launched into their awesome theme song.

"Stop!" the security guard shouted.

The Titans stood quietly while the man consulted his clipboard.

"You're not on the list," he said.

"But…" protested Robin. "We're super heroes!"

Just then, a purple-jumpsuit-wearing group of super heroes walked to the end of the red carpet.

"Hello," said one of them. "We're here for the motion picture."

The security guard looked at his clipboard.

"Right this way," he said, motioning to the group to walk past him.

"They're on the list?" asked Cyborg with disbelief. "We don't even know who they are!"

"*No* one knows them!" yelled Beast Boy.

BLAM!

The security guard stepped into the theater and slammed the door behind him. The Teen Titans stood on the red carpet in shock.

"Man, how's we supposed to get in now?" asked Beast Boy.

"I do have the ability to open portals to any feasible location," offered Raven.

"Oh yeah, that's right," said Robin. "Always forget about that. Portal it is!"

ZAAAAP!

One Raven-demonic-magic-portal-spell later, the Titans stood inside the movie theater.

"Aw, man, there's no seats!" observed Cyborg.

Raven pointed toward the seats taken by the purple-clad nobodies.

"Uh, what about those?" she asked.

"But that's where those nameless guys are sitting," said Robin.

"Dude, *no* one's gonna miss *them*!" argued Cyborg.

"Yeah, no one knows who they are!" agreed Beast Boy.

"Exactly," confirmed Starfire.

ZAAAAP!

Raven opened another portal, and the no-names were instantly sucked into it.

The portal closed, and the Teen Titans took the only empty seats in the theater.

A tall woman strode confidently to the front of the theater. She had white-blond hair, and she was casually yet stylishly dressed. When she stood in front of the screen, the crowd instantly grew quiet.

"Whoa, that's Jade Wilson, the famous movie director!" said Robin.

"Thank you, thank you all for coming to the premiere," said Jade Wilson. "Now, who's ready for a Batman movie?!"

Ecstatic cheers from the audience filled the theater.

"Good, good!" said Jade. "But first, I'd like to give you a sneak peek at some of our upcoming super hero movies!"

"Upcoming?" asked Robin with excitement.

"That's right!" said Jade. "We've decided to move on from Batman and really flesh out the cinematic universe. Starting, of course, with Batman's own supporting cast."

The theater lights began to dim. Robin squirmed in his seat, anxiously waiting for the preview to start.

"Supporting cast?" he said. "*I'm* part of Batman's supporting cast! They're finally going to make a movie about me!"

As the preview started, an announcer's voice loudly declared, "Coming this summer…"

"My movie is happening that soon?" wondered Robin with astonishment.

The announcer continued, "*Alfred: The Movie!*"

Suddenly, the screen was filled with the image of an elderly British man pushing a vacuum cleaner over a carpet in Wayne Manor. It was Alfred, Batman's loyal butler.

"It's time to clean up this city!" Alfred declared heroically as he ran the vacuum. "That's how you clean up a mess!" he quipped.

Beast Boy leaned closer to Robin and said, "Yo, don't worry, bro. If Alfred got a movie, you *must* be next!"

Robin thought about it for a moment and then said, "You're right! My movie must be slated for *next* summer!"

The announcer's voice continued, "Coming *next* summer..."

Robin closed his eyes and whispered from his seat, "Please be me, please be me, *please* be me!"

"You know the car!" said the announcer. "Equipped to avert any obstacle. Destroy any foe. And always gets the girl. *The Batmobile Rises.* Coming soon!"

Cyborg turned to Robin and said, "*Ohh*, they did the car before you, bro."

Robin gritted his teeth and muttered, "*Grrr*, this is ridiculous!"

"That Batmobile movie actually does look pretty good," said Raven.

"I'd go see it," said Beast Boy.

"I do love the Batman's automobile," Starfire added.

Robin glared at the screen and said, "They must be saving the best for last, then. I'm sure my movie is next *next* summer!"

"Coming next *next* summer!" said the announcer. "The story of Batman's greatest ally—"

A smile filled Robin's face, and he said, "That's me! That must be me!"

The announcer's voice rang out, "And best friend in the whole wide world."

"Finally!" said Robin. He jumped out of his seat and ran to the front of the theater. He stood below the movie screen to face the audience.

"Thank you, thank you for making a movie about—" he began.

"*Utility Belt: The Movie*," said the announcer.

Robin spun around to glare at the screen. A giant image of Batman's yellow Utility Belt filled the screen.

"*What?!*" yelled Robin.

The audience burst into laughter. The other super heroes were having a great time making fun of Robin—loudly.

"Ha-ha! He thought the movie was about *him*!" said one.

"What a joke! He's just a *sidekick*!" said another.

Choking back a sob, Robin ran as fast as he could out of the theater. His teammates ran after him.

Outside the theater, the Teen Titans gathered around Robin, trying to console him.

"Aw, man, forget those fools," said Beast Boy.

"Who cares what other people think?" asked Raven.

"We have the each other," added Starfire. "And that is all that matters."

"Star's right, bro," agreed Cyborg. "What do those big-shot super heroes know, anyway?"

Robin shook his head sadly and said, "They

know that having a movie is the only way to be seen as a real hero."

"You *are* the real hero to us!" said Starfire.

"Yeah," said Cyborg. "You put this team together!"

"Without you, we'd be all alone," added Raven.

"That's right!" said Beast Boy. "Without you, bro, I'd be living in a dumpster, eating garbage!"

"And I'd have to enslave entire dimensions with my evil dad," added Raven. "Yuck!"

"And I would be forced to return to my life of fighting in the pit of the intergalactic gladiator," said Starfire.

"And I'd be playing professional football," said Cyborg. "Oh, sure. Playing professional football *sounds* good…but you're forgetting the concussions, the bad knees, going broke, and having to be on one of them awful dance reality TV shows."

Robin, who was not paying attention to his teammates, said, "But why *don't* they take us seriously? We've got the cool costumes, the gadgets, the powers, and the sweet kung-fu moves! What are we *missing*?"

"Well, what about an archnemesis?" asked Raven.

"An archnemesis?" asked Robin.

"Oh yeah, an archnemesis is like a status symbol in the hero world," said Raven.

"Yeah, bro," agreed Cyborg. "Every super hero's got one."

"Super-bad dudes, with super-scary names," said Beast Boy.

"That are fun to say in the dramatic way!" agreed Starfire.

"Superman's got Lex Luthor!" said Cyborg.

"Ooo," said the other Titans simultaneously. *"Lex Luthor!"*

"Green Lantern's got Sinestro," said Beast Boy.

"Ooo," said the Titans simultaneously again. *"Sinestro!"*

"And The Flash has the Rainbow Raider," said Starfire. "He rides upon the rainbows."

The Titans were silent.

"An archnemesis *is* pretty scary," said Raven. "If you can get a crazed lunatic to devote himself to taking you down, it means you really are a top hero. You know, the kind they make movies about."

Robin pondered this for a moment and then said, "How do we get an archnemesis?"

BEEP! BEEP! BEEP!

Beast Boy reached into his pocket and removed a flashing communicator.

"It's a crime alert," he said.

"A crime alert?" said Robin with excitement. "It's a mysterious figure breaking into S.T.A.R. Labs. This could be it! The key to a movie about *me*!"

"Well, wouldn't that be convenient?" muttered Raven.

Robin was already running down the street.

"Titans, let's go get ourselves an archnemesis!" he called out to his teammates.

CHAPTER 3

Not far away, at the edge of the city of Metropolis, stood the world-famous scientific laboratory known as S.T.A.R. Labs. It had some of the tightest security in the world, but today an intruder had broken into the lab. The deadly villain Slade had dramatically crashed through the main entrance and thrown a smoke bomb in front of the lab's guards. He now stood in the middle of the lab, holding a sword in one hand. His head was entirely covered by a thick blue-and-orange mask, and he wore a dark-blue costume that was layered with protective armor. One evil eye glared through the mask.

"You won't get away with this," said one of the guards as he fell to the floor and inhaled the dangerous gas. "The…Justice…League…will stop… you," he gasped.

As the guard lost consciousness, Slade let out a sinister laugh.

"Sorry, my pathetic friend, but the Justice League won't be coming," said Slade, moving deeper into the lab. "Because they're watching a movie. And as considerate moviegoers, I'm sure they would have turned their telephones, communicators, and various crime alerts and whatnots off!"

Inside the darkened lab, Slade paused to admire a laser projector sitting on a pedestal. He slowly reached one hand toward the device.

WHAM!

A Birdarang zoomed through the lab and crashed into Slade's outstretched hand.

"Ouch!" he cried.

The Teen Titans charged into the lab.

"Stop right there, um, Ninja Guy?" called out Robin.

"I'm *not* a ninja," said Slade with a sigh.

"What?" asked Beast Boy with surprise. "You got them swords!"

"Lots of people have swords, okay?" said Slade

with frustration. "On the way here I passed, like, twenty-five people with swords."

Cyborg shook his head and said, "Nah, I'm pretty sure you're a weird version of a ninja."

Slade stamped his foot on the floor and said, "I'm *not*! I am the greatest! Most feared! Most nefarious! Most ultimate super-villain the world has ever seen! I . . . am . . . *Slade*!"

"Slade!" said Robin dramatically. "Wow, his name is really fun to say dramatically!"

"Slade," muttered Raven.

"Slade!" shouted Beast Boy and Starfire.

"Slllalallalaaaadddeeee," bellowed Cyborg.

"Silence!" said Slade angrily. "What is the *point* of all of this?"

"We're in need of an archnemesis, and we think you'd be a great fit!" explained Robin.

Slade uttered a scornful laugh and said, "Great fit? Oh, I'm sorry. Just one second, please. *Archnemesis?* To the *Teeny Titans?* You gotta be kidding me!"

He glared at the heroes and continued, "I mean,

archnemesis to Batman? *Sure!* Archnemesis to Superman? That's more like it! But you guys are a joke! *Everyone* knows that! Now get out of my way. I'm not interested in fighting a bunch of sidekicks and half a robot!"

"Oh, you want *real* super heroes?" asked Raven.

"We'll *show* you real super heroes!" said Cyborg.

"Titans, *GO!*" shouted Robin.

On Robin's command, the five Titans soared through the air and crashed into Slade. The villain was quickly knocked to the floor of the lab.

"Impressive work, Titans!" said Robin with a smile. "Was *that* real enough for you, Slade?"

"Ha! Child's play," said Slade as he stood up and faced the Titans. "That little fight allowed me to analyze your interpersonal dynamics and psychological profiles. Now the *true* battle begins. And you've already lost! Because no one can withstand my powers of *mind manipulation!*"

Robin crossed his arms and declared smugly, "We aren't falling for any mind-manipulation tactics!"

"I'll make you think twice about that!" replied Slade. "I'll warp your concept of reality *and* bend the parameters of space and time, destroying the logic of your world in a matter of seconds!"

Robin yawned and replied, "Prove it."

Slade reached into a pocket and produced a pencil.

"Look at *this*!" he declared dramatically. "Behold an ordinary pencil, made of rigid wood and graphite, held together by a polymer adhesive. Topped off with a delightful eraser."

"And what's your point?" asked Beast Boy.

"Can a solid pencil…do *this*?" asked Slade. He wiggled the pencil between his fingers so quickly that it looked as if it was bending.

"Oh my gosh!" said an awestruck Beast Boy. "The pencil…it's all rubbery and—"

Before Beast Boy could finish his sentence, Slade bent one thumb behind the palm of his hand.

"The pencil is just the start of it," Slade interrupted. "You may think you have a grasp on reality, but how can you even begin to explain this?"

Slade waved his hand in the air. Because of the way he was holding his hand, it looked like his thumb had disappeared.

"Yes, an ordinary opposable *thumb*," said Slade with a sinister laugh. "Connected by flesh, tendons, and muscles. But what you are witnessing may very well pull the rug of empirical science from underneath your feet!"

"*Eeek!* His thumb...it's *gone*!" cried the horrified Titans.

Robin blinked and shook his head. With a frown, he declared, "Wait a minute. These are just tricks and optical illusions!"

Slade motioned behind Robin and frantically pointed toward the back of the lab.

"Whoa! Oh my gosh!" he said. "What's that over there behind you? What's *that*?"

"Don't listen to him!" declared Robin. "He's just trying to trick you again! It's absolutely nothing!"

Slade shook his head and shouted, "Oh my gosh! No, seriously! I've never...what is that? Is that even a—"

"Don't turn around and look, Titans!" commanded Robin. "There is *nothing* over there!"

"Even if *one* of you looks and the other ones close your eyes!" suggested Slade.

"There's probably nothing over there!" insisted Robin. "He's lying!"

The other four Titans strained to not turn their heads and look behind them.

"Look, guys," implored Slade. "I'm serious! *Look!*"

Robin closed his eyes and planted his feet more firmly on the ground. He strained every muscle, fighting the urge to turn his head.

"I...I can't resist!" said Robin. "Must...look...*behind* me!"

The Teen Titans couldn't hold out any longer. All five heroes turned around. As soon as they did that, Slade grabbed the laser projector and ran away.

"Hey, what the...?" protested Cyborg.

"There's nothing there!" observed Beast Boy.

"He tricked the us," said Starfire sadly.

From outside S.T.A.R. Labs, the voice of Slade floated down the hallway as he escaped.

"See ya later, losers!" he called out. "Gimme a call when you guys learn how to be real super heroes!"

Robin sighed and turned to face his teammates.

"He's right," he said sadly. "We're *not* real super heroes. They'll never make a movie about us!"

Later that afternoon, the heroes were hanging out in the skyscraper known as Titans Tower, their team headquarters. Robin sulked in his bedroom. He was remembering every insulting comment that the other super heroes had made about him earlier that day.

"Calling me a joke," Robin muttered angrily. "Calling me a goofster. Saying I'm just a sidekick..."

Before he could finish the list of insults, his teammates burst into his room. Beast Boy was carrying a large cardboard box.

"Yo, Robin," said Beast Boy. "Come check this out, my man!"

"Not now, Beast Boy," said Robin with a frown. "I'm *not* in the mood."

Beast Boy reached out to grab Robin and pushed the Boy Wonder into the cardboard box.

"Trust me, dude," said Beast Boy. "You're not gonna wanna be late for this!"

Robin sighed. "What are you talking about? Why am I sitting in this cardboard box?"

"It's a limo, dude!" replied Beast Boy, pushing the cardboard box containing Robin into the living room.

"What the—?" sputtered Robin.

When they reached the living room, Robin saw the other Titans gathered around the TV.

"Here we are," said Beast Boy. He grabbed Robin and pulled him from the cardboard box. "Let me help you with the door."

"*What* are you guys doing?" Robin asked.

Cyborg stepped forward and shoved Robin onto the couch.

"Have a seat, my dude!" said Cyborg.

Raven handed Robin a box of candy and said, "Don't forget your favorite snack."

Starfire placed a bag of popcorn in Robin's other hand. "And the corn of popping!" she said.

"Now sit back and relax, and enjoy *Robin: The Movie!*" Cyborg said, and turned on the TV.

The sound of an announcer's voice came from

the TV. The announcer sounded just like Beast Boy. Well, actually it was Beast Boy doing an announcer impression.

"Yo, this is the story about a dude," said the announcer. "And this is not a ordinary dude, no, sir. This dude gots a name, and it's . . . *Robin*!"

A crudely drawn title card filled the screen. It read *"Robin: The Movie."*

"Yaaaay!" shouted Robin's teammates.

Suddenly, the screen was filled with bouncing stick puppets. One of the poorly made puppets was a very young Robin, who was wearing a circus acrobat's costume.

The announcer's voice continued, "Robin was just a little baby boy that lived at the circus. Doin' acrobatics and things."

Robin squirmed on the couch.

"C'mon, guys," he said. "This is *embarrassing*!"

"Shhhh," said Cyborg.

The announcer said, "But then he grew up, and he wasn't a baby no more!"

Robin grimaced in response to this, watching the camera zoom in on the Robin stick puppet's hands.

"But he still had them baby hands, yo," continued the announcer.

Starfire clapped her hands together and said, "Coming up is the part that is the best!"

Robin jumped off the couch. He marched over to the TV and quickly turned it off.

"This is ridiculous, guys!" he complained.

"Hey!" protested Beast Boy. "We worked hard on that, yo!"

"We were just trying to cheer you up," said Raven.

Robin glared at his teammates and replied, "By making *fun* of me?"

"Perhaps if you continue to watch—" began Starfire.

"No!" declared Robin. "I want a *real* movie!"

"Then let's just go get one!" suggested Cyborg.

"Oh, like it's that easy," said Robin as he shook his head sadly. "We gotta face it, guys! No one's gonna make a movie about us. We're just a joke!"

Cyborg wrapped his arm around Robin's shoulder and said, "You know what you need? You need an upbeat inspirational song about life!"

With that, the Titans launched into an inspirational song about life, just for Robin.

At the end of the incredibly inspirational song, Robin jumped into the air and shouted, "I feel like I can do anything!"

"Inspirational music does that," confirmed Cyborg.

"I *can* get my own movie!" declared Robin. *"Hollywood, here we come!"*

"Road trip!" shouted the other Titans. They tumbled into the elevator and descended to the Titans Tower garage.

Seconds later, the team was crammed into the T-Car. They were headed to Hollywood, singing an upbeat road song—

WHAM! CRASH! SPLAT!

Before they could finish the tune, the T-Car ran over the rock band that had been dutifully providing the upbeat instrumental backing for their song.

"Oops," said Robin as he hit the brakes.

The Titans peered over the edge of the car to survey the damage.

"How about if I just open a portal?" suggested Raven.

"Yeah, that's a wise move," replied Beast Boy.

"We probably *should* get outta here," added Cyborg.

ZAAAP!

Raven magically created a portal in the middle of the road. The Titans quickly jumped into it, successfully fleeing the mess they were leaving behind.

The poor band stumbled around, trying their best to find the musical instruments the T-Car had destroyed.

CHAPTER 4

Seconds later, the Teen Titans emerged from the portal.
They had arrived in sunny Burbank, California.
They were standing on a sidewalk on Warner Boulevard, just steps away from the main entrance to
the world-famous Warner Bros. Studios.

Robin looked longingly at the studio's tan-colored buildings and tall sound stages.

"There it is: the studio!" he said. "Once we pass
through these gates, our lives will change forever!
Now, Titans! Are you ready to be movie stars?"

The group smiled and marched to the entrance.
Before they could enter the studio, though, a security guard reached out his long arm to stop them.
It was the same guard from the Batman movie
premiere. He was carrying the same clipboard.

"And just who are you?" he asked.

"Ugh, this guy, really?" muttered Raven.

Robin chuckled confidently and said, "You don't remember us?"

"This fool don't remember us!" said Beast Boy with a laugh.

"Perhaps this song will remind you," said Cyborg, grabbing his cassette and preparing to lead the team in their awesome theme song.

Before they could sing a note, the guard slammed his hand on his clipboard.

"Stop!" he shouted. "You're *not* on the list!"

The team retreated a few steps away from the entrance.

"Great, *now* how are we supposed to get in?" asked Robin.

"Portal?" suggested Raven.

"Oh yeah, good idea," agreed the other Titans.

One portal later, the Titans found themselves inside the Warner Bros. Studios lot.

"A real-life studio!" said Robin happily. "We're standing on the back lot! This is where the magic happens!"

"Look at all those fancy Porta Potties over there!" marveled Beast Boy.

"Don't be fooled by the glitz and glamour," warned Raven. "If we let our guard down, Hollywood will tear us apart."

Robin led the team past the first of several large sound stages.

"Come on, everyone," he said. "Jade Wilson is in one of these sound stages. But which one? This place is so big and confusing. If only we had some sort of guide."

Suddenly, a famous magical wizard materialized in front of the Titans.

"If it's guidance you seek, I can provide it," he intoned sagely.

"Yeah, okay, thanks," said Robin as the Titans walked past the wizard. "That's great and all, but we're just looking for—"

Just then, another famous star waddled up to them and began to offer *his* sage advice.

"Hey, yo, yo!" said Cyborg with a sigh. "Can you all chill with the cautionary wisdom? Huh?"

"Yeah, fools," agreed Beast Boy. "We just wanna know where Jade Wilson is."

The wizard replied, "Oh, right. She's right over there at Stage 52."

"Thanks, dude," said Beast Boy.

"Weirdos," muttered Robin.

The Titans cautiously opened the metal door outside of Stage 52 and entered the massive building. Their mouths opened in awe. There was Jade Wilson. She was sitting in a director's chair, and she was directing a big-budget super hero movie.

"Whoa, rad, check it out!" whispered Beast Boy.

"Quiet on the set!" called out Jade. "Lights! Cameras! *Batman v Superman: Part Two.* Action!"

WHAP!

Someone snapped the two parts of a clapboard together. Two costumed actors portraying Superman and Batman walked slowly toward each other. They both had grim and gritty expressions on their faces.

"What's your mother's name?" demanded Batman grimly.

"Martha," came Superman's gritty reply.

"My mom's name is Martha, too," said Batman as he slowly softened his expression, realizing he had something important in common with his foe. "Wait...what's your father's name?"

"Jonathan," said Superman angrily.

"Mine's Thomas!" replied Batman furiously.

BLAM! POW! CRASH!

With even grimmer and grittier looks of hatred, Superman and Batman started punching each other.

"Cut!" yelled Jade. "Excellent work, everyone! Take five, and we'll go again."

"Those performances were the amazing!" said Starfire to the other Titans.

Beast Boy turned to Robin and asked, "Well, what are you waiting for, bro?"

"Go the forth, Robin," urged Starfire. "The destiny awaits!"

Suddenly, Robin seemed somewhat unsure of himself.

"Um, do you really think she's going to give me a movie?" he asked.

"*Give?*" said Cyborg. "When Batman wants vengeance, do bad guys just give it to him?"

"Well, no . . ." admitted Robin.

"That's *right*!" declared Cyborg. "Batman *takes* that vengeance, all crackin' skulls and puttin' fools in the hospital!"

"Leaving them with the permanent injuries," added Starfire.

"It's the same with movies," said Raven. "She won't just give you a movie; you have to take it!"

"Now, *what* do you want?" Cyborg asked.

"A movie," replied Robin timidly.

"Say it *loud*!" encouraged Beast Boy.

"I want a movie!" Robin said, a bit more enthusiastically.

"Again!" said Starfire.

"I want a *movie*!" shouted Robin.

"Then take it!" suggested Raven.

"*I'm gonna take it!*" Robin screamed at the top of his lungs.

With a determined look on his face, Robin marched up to Jade.

"Hey! Jade Wilson!" he called out confidently.

Jade put down her script and peered sternly at Robin. His confidence evaporated.

"Um," he said nervously, "would you please make a movie about me?"

Jade sat back in her chair with a thoughtful look on her face.

"A movie about you?" she said. "Why don't you tell me about it?"

That was all the prompting Robin needed to sell her on *Robin: The Movie.*

"It would be so awesome," he said, jumping from one foot to the other with excitement. "It would be *so* cool, it would be the most amazing and successful super hero movie ever with special effects, like tons and tons of special effects, and my super-sweet cape would blow your mind. Oh and I'd have my own hero music, too, it'd go *bum-bum-bum-bum-bum-bum-bum-bum-boom*; my sweet and ominous catchphrase would be, 'Traffic report—criminals... expect delays—'"

Panting with exhaustion, Robin paused to catch his breath. Jade closed her eyes for a moment. She was considering his proposal. She opened her eyes.

"No," she said.

Robin's mouth drooped into a frown.

"Why *can't* I have a movie?" he asked.

"You're a joke," replied Jade. "The Teen Titans are a joke. Making a movie about you would be a waste of good film. In fact, the only way I'd even consider it is if you were the only super heroes left in the universe. Good day!"

With that, she pointed to the exit. Robin and the other Teen Titans reluctantly left the sound stage.

"I am sorry, friend Robin," said Starfire.

Robin had a big smile on his face, and he quickly replied, "Don't be sorry!"

"You're taking this surprisingly well," observed Raven.

"Of *course* I am!" said Robin. "Didn't you hear what she said?"

"That we are the jokes?" asked Starfire.

"That making a movie about us would be a waste of film?" added Cyborg.

"No!" said Robin. "That she would make a movie about us if we were the only super heroes around! So all we have to do is..."

Robin paused dramatically to let another Titan finish his sentence.

"Kill all the other super heroes?" asked Raven.

"*Close*, but no!" replied Robin. "I want us to save them from becoming super heroes *in the first place*!"

Robin reached into his Utility Belt and removed an easel and a large chart. There were several panels of drawings showing the origin stories of Superman, Batman, and other super heroes.

"These graphics will explain my plan," he said. "I propose we travel through time and stop those tragic events from taking place."

"Robin, this is the *excellent* plan!" said Starfire.

"Great idea, dude," added Beast Boy. "Let's do some time travelin', yo!"

"To the Time Cycles!" Robin dramatically called out.

"Time Cycles?" Raven asked. "What's wrong with our usual time machine?"

"It's boring!" said Robin. "We need something more cinematic! Raven, summon the Time Cycles!"

"Fine," replied Raven. *"Azarath…Metrion… Zinthos!"*

POOF!

Magically, five Time Cycles appeared. Each had a giant wheel in front, a low-set seat, and two smaller wheels in the rear. There were even sparkly tassels hanging from the handlebars, each one matching the color scheme for one of the heroes so nobody got confused. The Titans jumped onto the bikes, but the vehicles refused to move.

"Man, these bikes ain't got no power!" protested Beast Boy.

Robin replied, "These Time Cycles are powered by *radness*. Are you ready?"

The other Titans nodded in agreement.

Robin declared, "Then let's go to the past!"

Cyborg placed a cassette tape into a panel on his metallic chest. Suddenly, *extremely* rad and *totally* awesome music filled the air. The bikes began to move, but not very fast.

"We're not rad enough, bro!" observed Beast Boy.

"Titans! Deploy time streamers!" commanded Robin. *"Engage!"*

Bright, rainbow-hued blasts of color shot out of the back of the Time Cycles. With that, the Titans reached peak radness and broke through the space-time barrier. Soon, they were zooming through a time tunnel. "We did it!" called out Robin. "We breached the space-time continuum with our radness! First stop: Superman!"

In a faraway galaxy, the planet Krypton was dying. Earthquakes were rumbling; steam geysers were blasting through the ground. The famous Kryptonian scientist Jor-El knew that the planet was doomed. He and his wife, Lara, were standing in his laboratory. In her arms was their infant son, Kal-El.

BEEP! BEEP! BEEP!

A digital display at a command console was urgently flashing red. A set of green crystals embedded in the shaking console began to crack.

"There is no time left," said Jor-El. "Our planet is about to explode. We can save our son, Kal-El, by placing him in this spaceship and sending him to Earth, where he will be safe."

"Good-bye, my beloved son," said Lara, caressing her son for the last time.

BLAM!

The Teen Titans burst into the lab.

"Whoa, whoa, whoa, whoa!" yelled Robin. "Hold it right there!"

Jor-El looked up with puzzlement and said, "But…"

"You are the *horrible* parents!" scolded Starfire.

"Yeah. Shooting a baby into space?" added Raven. "What kinda people are you?"

"But we have no choice!" said Jor-El, pointing to the flashing display. "The crystals are not harmonized. The planet is collapsing! I've tried all of the combinations!"

"Fool, if you wanna save the planet, you gots to play the right music!" said Beast Boy.

"Yeah," agreed Cyborg. "Let us show you how it's done!"

The five Titans positioned themselves at the console and started touching the crystals. Their movements on the crystals created a beat so totally awesome that the planet's destruction was avoided.

"*That's* what's up!" said Beast Boy.

"Aw, yeah," said Cyborg. "We did it! Hope you enjoyed the show!"

Robin hopped back on his Time Cycle and called out, "Now let's go stop some more super hero origins!"

Seconds later, the Teen Titans disappeared into the Time Tunnel.

It was a dark and gloomy night in Gotham City. A happy family had just departed from the Monarch movie theater, where they had seen *The Mask of Zorro*. The two parents, Thomas and Martha Wayne, were both well-dressed. Their young son, Bruce, was waving an imaginary sword in the air, pretending to be the masked hero in the movie he had just seen.

"Come on, let's take this shortcut," Thomas Wayne said as he led his wife and son toward a dimly lit alleyway. A shadowy figure could be seen moving ominously at the end of the alley.

BLAM!

The Teen Titans burst onto the dark street in front of the Wayne family.

"Whoa, stop!" Robin called out. "You can't go down there!"

"That is *Crime Alley*, you dum-dums!" shouted Cyborg.

"May I suggest that you take a shortcut through Happy Lane, instead?" suggested Starfire.

As the Wayne family looked on in amazement, the Titans took off again on their Time Cycles.

About an hour later, the Titans returned triumphantly to the streets of Burbank to celebrate the completion of their mission.

They had prevented Superman and Batman from existing. They had also visited Themyscira and taken away young Diana's Lasso of Truth. They had stopped Hal Jordan from discovering a damaged spaceship that contained a member of the Green Lantern Corps.

"Well, we made it," said Robin with a smile.

"We're back in the present and there are no more super heroes."

BRRRRRING!

Suddenly, an alarm sounded down the street. The Titans looked over to see a group of super-villains running from a bank. Not far away, another group of villains had set fire to a police station. In the studio behind them, they could see yet another set of villains ripping apart the famous Warner Bros. water tower.

"What happened, yo?" asked a puzzled Beast Boy.

"Without super heroes, the world seems to have become a horrific wasteland, overrun by villains," observed Cyborg.

"But are they still making super hero movies?" Robin asked hopefully.

Raven consulted the news reports on her phone and replied, "No movies. Only suffering."

Robin sighed with frustration and hopped back on his Time Cycle.

"Titans!" he called out. "Back to the past!"

And so the Titans began their journey to undo their undoings of the origin stories of the world's most famous super heroes.

CHAPTER 5

The Titans found themselves standing outside Stage 52 on the Warner Bros. Studios lot. They were back where—and when—they had started.

"Well, altering the space-time continuum didn't work," said Cyborg.

"So, you can say it was a waste of *time*," said Raven with a chuckle. "Ha-ha. That's pretty funny."

Robin ignored Raven and said, "Then we have no choice, Titans. We have to prove to Jade Wilson that we're not a joke."

"How's we gonna do that?" asked Beast Boy.

BEEP! BEEP! BEEP!

Robin reached into his pocket and removed his flashing communicator.

"With this crime alert from the observatory, that's how," he said. "It's Slade!"

"*Slaaaaaaade,*" said the other Titans with awe.

"Stop that!" said Robin peevishly. "If we can make Slade our archnemesis, then Jade Wilson will see that we're worthy of a movie. So no songs, no jokes, and whatever you do, don't fall prey to Slade's mind manipulation!"

The other Titans shrugged and nodded in agreement.

"Titans, *GO!*" Robin yelled, and ran down the street. His teammates were right behind him.

Across town, at the observatory, there was a solitary light in a room. Slade held a flashlight in one hand. His other hand was cautiously reaching toward a shining lens that was located within a high-tech telescope.

"I must be careful now!" he said. "That lens is made of pure crystallized itronium, one of the rarest elements on Earth. Without it, my doomsday device will be useless."

Ever so slowly, he removed the lens from the telescope.

"At last, my plan will be complete," he said, "and I will—"

These are the Teen Titans!

They're the coolest super heroes in Jump City. It's their job to protect their home from any potential evildoers who threaten it.

Today Jump City is being attacked by Balloon Man! He's huge and has a bunch of menacing balloon animals that help him terrorize the city.

The Teen Titans appear, but Balloon Man says he doesn't know who they are! He's not interested in fighting them.

The Justice League arrives to help. They can sort of see where Balloon Man is coming from. The Justice League is off to see the new Batman movie. He's a *real* hero. How can the Teen Titans be *real* super heroes if they don't even have a movie?

The Titans have to sneak in to see the Batman movie. All the big super heroes are there!

Robin isn't happy. *Everyone* else has their own movie, even Batman's Batmobile!

Robin knows what has to happen if the team is going to be taken seriously as heroes. To get the Titans the recognition they deserve, they need to star in a movie of their own!

The gang heads to Hollywood. Everything is awesome there—the sets, the costumes, and especially the celebrities!

They meet Jade Wilson. She's one of the best directors in Hollywood, so naturally they want her to direct their movie.

But Jade says she wouldn't direct their movie if the
Teen Titans were the last super heroes on earth!

The last super heroes on earth, huh?
The Titans can find a way to arrange that....

Meanwhile, a mysterious super-villain named Slade appears and has an even more mysterious plan. The Titans will have to foil his scheme.

Slade attempts a daring robbery. The Titans face off against him, but he's so strong! And so cunning! And so evil!

Will the team be able to save the world *and* their movie? There's only one way to find out.

Before he could finish his sentence, a voice called out to him.

"Drop that lens!" commanded Robin.

Slade spun around to see the Teen Titans standing at the doorway.

"Well, well. If it isn't the Teeny Titans," said Slade with a sneer. "I see you all are gluttons for punishment."

Robin clasped his fists together and replied, "The party's over, Slade!"

"Slaaaaaaade," said the other Titans with awe.

"Wrong!" yelled Slade. "The party has actually just begun! And I'm about to thoroughly enjoy disposing of your inferior intellects. With *mind manipulation*! While I am typically not a man of sympathy, I will pity you fools after I finish eviscerating your vacuous little skulls!"

Slade pointed behind the Titans.

"Oh my gosh," he cried out. *"What's going on over there?!"*

The Titans smiled in defiance and refused to turn around.

"It's a wall," replied Raven.

"Oh, okay," said Slade with disappointment. "Yes, it *is* a wall. Um, one second, please."

Slade pondered this setback and then tried again.

"I see you've managed to decipher one of my simpler mind manipulations that are usually reserved for babies," he taunted. "But try—if you dare—to explain the freakish mind bomb that is this!"

With that, he pulled a piece of paper out of his pocket. It showed two parallel lines shaped like arrows.

"The lines are of equal length!" he said triumphantly. "And yet they appear to be different lengths! One looks longer than the other! Explain that!"

"It's an optical illusion created by Müller-Lyer," replied Raven.

"Put it to rest, Slade!" said Robin. "We're not falling for your mind tricks anymore!"

"Okay," said Slade sadly. "I am noble enough to admit when I'm wrong. And, oh my, would you look at *that*? What's that on your shirt right there?"

"Give it up, Slade! It's game over!"

"That's what you think," said Slade. "Perhaps

at this present time it's best for me to use a more physical approach!"

Slade removed a laser-blaster from his pocket and fired it.

KER-BLAM!

The weapon blew a hole in a nearby window. Slade then tossed a wire cable through the hole. Before the Titans could react, he soared through the air and disappeared from view. He was holding the lens tight in his hand.

"Titans, *GO!*" commanded Robin.

Within seconds, Cyborg reassembled his bionic body parts. He converted his metallic arms into two giant laser cannons. His legs transformed into powerful jet engines, and his back changed into a bodyglider large enough for Robin and Beast Boy to climb on board. Cyborg and his passengers zoomed through the hole in the ceiling, and Starfire and Raven were not far behind.

"Steady, we've got him boxed in," yelled Robin as he aimed Cyborg's laser cannons toward Slade. "Ready...aim...*fire!*"

BLAM! BLAM! BLAM!

As the Titans watched in dismay, Cyborg's mighty cannon blasts destroyed the famous HOLLYWOOD sign on a nearby hill and missed Slade completely.

"Oops," said Robin.

Suddenly, the air was filled with helicopters from local TV stations. Each one started broadcasting the fight between Slade and the Teen Titans on their evening news shows.

"Our on-site news chopper has captured some remarkable footage out by the Hollywood sign," said one reporter.

"Five unidentified flying super heroes are in pursuit of a masked villain," said another.

"We take you live to this spectacular pursuit in progress!" said yet another.

Meanwhile, Robin was bouncing up and down as Cyborg swerved through the air.

"I can't get a clean shot," he complained.

Beast Boy was perched on top of Cyborg's head. Thinking quickly, Beast Boy transformed into a squirrel.

"We got this," he yelled.

"Yeah, we do!" confirmed Cyborg. He detached his mechanical head and launched it toward Slade. Squirrel–Beast Boy held on tight as he flew through the air.

"Over here!" squeaked Beast Boy. "Can't catch me!"

Slade spun around in confusion. That allowed Raven to swoop close to the villain.

"Got it," she said, grabbing the lens from Slade's hand.

Raven instantly opened a portal and transported herself back to Titans Tower. She landed in front of the team's super-secure vault, reached up to the vault's control panel, and entered the secret vault code.

BEEP! BOOP! BEEP!

As the vault's door popped open, a mechanical voice responded, "Vault access granted."

Raven placed the lens inside the vault and quickly closed the door. She then hopped back into the portal to rejoin the aerial fight between her teammates and Slade. Beast Boy was still atop Cyborg's head. Robin was piloting Cyborg's body-glider.

"The lens is secure!" announced Raven.

"You'll *never* get it now, Slade," said Robin. "No one can penetrate our vault! Nice job, Titans!"

The Titans paused to celebrate their victory in midair with high fives all around. Then they looked behind them and saw that Slade had two giant laser cannons pointed directly at them.

ZZZZZZAP! ZZZZZZAP!

Red-hot laser rays shot through the air and smashed into Cyborg's head. The head and Beast Boy both fell through the sky.

Robin called out, "Raven, Starfire! Go after them! I'll take care of Slade!"

With just moments to spare, Starfire and Raven swooped in and caught Cyborg's head and Beast Boy, bringing them safely to the ground.

"You saved me!" said Beast Boy happily.

A smile filled Cyborg's face, and then he looked down to see that his torso was missing.

"Hey, where's my body?" he cried.

BLAM!

Farther down the street, the Titans could see that Robin had crash-landed Cyborg's body-glider on top of Slade. The villain survived the impact, but Cyborg's torso was smashed into hundreds of small metallic chunks.

"Give it up, Slade!" declared Robin as he jumped to his feet and faced the villain.

"Impressive," admitted Slade. "You truly are a worthy...*archnemesis*."

Robin grinned with pleasure and said, "Archnemesis? *Really?* You mean it?"

"Indeed," replied Slade. "Like Batman and the Joker. Like Superman and Lex Luthor. Like The Flash and Rainbow Raider. I think you and I are destined to do this forever." Slade took a step back and declared, "Until next time, Robin...."

"There's not going to *be* a next time, Slade," declared Robin. "You're going to prison!"

Slade sighed and said, "That's *not* how having an archnemesis works! I get away, and you foil my next plan in an even more heroic way. It'll make a great movie."

Robin was temporarily distracted when he heard this.

"A movie...?" he pondered.

Lost in this thought, Robin didn't even notice as Slade quickly escaped.

"Hey, wait," said Robin. "Where did Slade go?"

The other Titans caught up to him. A look of anguish filled Cyborg's face as he viewed his ruined torso.

"Aw, *man*!" bellowed the Cyborg head. "What have you done? I'm *never* letting you fly my body again!"

"Where is the Slade?" asked Starfire.

"He got away," said Robin. "But we'll get him next time!"

As the Titans gathered up pieces of Cyborg's body, a crowd of pedestrians gathered around them. A few started to applaud, and others began to cheer.

"What's they doin', yo?" asked a puzzled Beast Boy.

"They're cheering…for us?" wondered Cyborg's detached head.

Starfire gasped and said, "Because we have done the hero things!"

ZOOOOM!

Just then, a long black limousine pulled up next to the Titans. Jade Wilson stepped out of the car.

"My darlings, you did it!" she said, walking over to the Teen Titans. "That battle with Slade? Ah! Electric!"

Robin blushed with pride and said, "Thanks, Miss Wilson. Just doing our jobs!"

"Now, I'm rarely ever wrong, but perhaps I've misjudged you guys," continued Jade. "What I'm getting at is that I want my next movie to star the Teen Titans!"

"You are aware that we are ordinary, unattractive people, right?" asked Cyborg.

"Oh yes, I know!" agreed Jade. "But that doesn't matter! I'm making the movie anyway! It's going to be about Robin, the leader, and the formation of the Teen Titans. And it's going to culminate in the triumphant victory over Slade!

"Now there's lots to do, so I have to run!" she said as she quickly stepped back into her limousine. "Meet me tomorrow morning, bright and early, at the movie studio. My ordinary-looking young movie stars, we've got *history* to make! Ta-ta!"

As Jade's limousine sped down the street, Robin closed his eyes and smiled.

"It's happening!" he said, "It's *really* happening!"

"Robin, your dream is coming the true!" said Starfire happily.

Robin jumped up in the air and yelled triumphantly, "The Teen Titans are getting their *movie*!"

CHAPTER 6

The next day found the Teen Titans once again standing on the sidewalk outside the Warner Bros. Studios lot.

"Titans, when we cross this gate, our lives will change forever," Robin said dramatically as he bounded toward the security guard at the gate. "Are you *ready*, Titans?"

His teammates nodded happily and walked behind him.

The security guard reached for his clipboard and peered at the new arrivals.

"Whoa, it's the Teen Titans!" he said enthusiastically. "Oh wow, oh wow, oh wow. This is an honor! You guys are the *best*!"

"You know who we are?" Robin asked with surprise.

"Yes, sir!" replied the guard. "You're on the list!"

The five Titans jumped in the air and smacked their hands together.

"We're on the list!" they yelled happily.

"Miss Wilson is waiting for you guys at sound stage 5," said the guard.

"That is the more like the it," said Starfire as the team marched in.

Robin was practically vibrating with excitement as the Titans walked to the door to sound stage 5 and entered the giant building. A perfect replica of the Titans Tower living room had been constructed in the middle of the sound stage. Giant lights and several motion picture cameras stood ready at the edge of the set.

As the Titans wandered around, Robin's mouth fell open in awe. "*Oooo*...wow...incredible!" he said happily. "It's really happening! This set seems so real!"

Jade Wilson walked over to join him and said, "Pretty magical, huh? We spared no expense."

"Miss Wilson, this is fantastic!" declared Robin. "It looks *just* like our real living room."

Robin walked toward the back of the set and said, "I'm going to go check out the bathroom."

"Well, the bathroom's not real," said Jade.

"Uh, yeah, it is. I pooped in it," said Beast Boy.

Jade looked down at Beast Boy in surprise and said, "Say again? You did *what* now?"

"I pooped in it!" confirmed Beast Boy.

Seconds later, Cyborg walked up to the group.

"Hoo, doggie!" he said with a laugh. "Do not go in the bathroom, cuz I just wrecked it, baby!"

"That's what's up!" agreed Beast Boy. He and Cyborg high-fived each other.

"We pooped in the toilet!" they both declared.

"*Stop* that!" said Jade with annoyance. "You are pooping in a prop toilet!"

"I dunno, bro," said Cyborg doubtfully. "It looked real to me."

"Yeah, looked real," confirmed Beast Boy.

Starfire then rejoined the group and said, "*Ahhh*, there is nothing quite like doing the poops in the new bathroom."

"She pooped in the toilet!" shouted Cyborg and Beast Boy.

"*No one* should be using that toilet!" said Jade angrily. "Look, you jackaloons! There is no plumbing. There is nowhere for the poops to go!"

71

From behind the prop bathroom door, Raven's voice called out, "Hey, will you keep it down out there? I'm trying to poop in here!"

"Aaaargh!" bellowed Jade.

Later that day, in the middle of a windowless and gloomy room that looked as if it would be perfect for a villain's lair, Slade sat in a large chair. He slammed his hand down on the chair's armrest and started to rant.

"Bested by teenagers!" he snarled. "And now the last piece of my device is locked up in their vault? It looks like they're stronger than I thought. No matter, though. All I need to do is divide...and conquer!"

With that, Slade held up a large photo of the Teen Titans. He then grabbed a sword and chopped the photo into five jagged pieces.

"After I have removed Robin's pesky teammates, it will be easy to use my mind manipulation on him," Slade said. "Robin will open the vault for me without even knowing it. And then the world will finally—"

Before he could finish his sentence, Robin and the other Titans bounded into the room.

"Not a chance, Slade!" declared Robin. "You'll never break us up! Titans, *GO!*"

The Titans ran to the chair and started pummeling the villain. Slade quickly jumped out of harm's way and removed his mask.

"Wait, wait!" he cried. "Hold on! I'm just an actor. It's just a mask!"

"Nice try, Slade, but we're not falling for that mind manipulation!" declared Robin. "We know you're the real Slade!"

"And the real Slade's about to get a beatdown!" Cyborg confirmed, grabbing the villain.

"No, no, no, no!" cried their opponent.

Suddenly, Jade Wilson's voice filled the air.

"Cut, cut!" she yelled. "You dimwits, this isn't a real fight! He's just an *actor*!"

"Yeah, I swear…I'm just an actor," confirmed the frightened man.

"Yeah, sure," said Beast Boy sarcastically, winking at the other Titans. "We get it. An *actor*, right?"

"*Get* him!" the five Titans yelled, and they started pummeling the frightened actor again.

"No, no, no, no!" screamed Jade. "Hold it, hold it!"

Robin looked up mid-pummel and asked, "What is it now?"

"Listen, guys," said Jade. "This is all fake! It's a bunch of phony-baloney. It's not real."

The Titans glanced at one another. They looked puzzled.

"It's all for pretend," she continued.

The Titans stared at her. They did not seem to understand.

"Oh my gosh! You people are idiots," said Jade with frustration.

"Wait, so you mean…none of this stuff is real?" Beast Boy said slowly. "Is that what you're saying?"

"Are you trying to say what we see isn't reality?" added Cyborg.

"It is the illusion?" wondered Starfire.

Jade nodded her head quickly and said, "Right.

Yeah, now you're getting it. None of this is real. It's all just an illusion, thanks to movie magic!"

"Oh wow, yeah!" said Robin. "I mean, I totally get it—it's props and make-believe, totally!"

Jade smiled and said, "I guess there might be hope for you idiots after all!"

"Hey, guys, no hard feelings," said the actor as he sat back down in the chair. "I know how some of this stuff can appear really real."

The actor smiled at the Titans and placed the mask over his head.

"Slade!" shouted Beast Boy.

"Get him!" yelled the other Titans, charging toward the frightened actor.

Jade Wilson buried her head in her hands and moaned with frustration.

Two hours later, Jade had finally convinced the Teen Titans that it was an actor inside the Slade costume. She also had threatened to cancel the movie if the Titans didn't shape up.

At the corner of the sound stage, Robin pleaded with his teammates.

"Please, this is my *dream*! We finally have a chance to show everyone how we're real heroes! Please, promise me you won't screw this up!"

"Sure, bro," replied Beast Boy.

"Whatever," said Raven.

"Thank you!" said Robin, and a smile filled his face. "Okay, Miss Wilson, they're ready!"

"Fantastic!" said Jade. "Okay, Titans. Take your place on the set. In this new scene, Slade has kidnapped and tied up four of the Titans—Cyborg, Beast Boy, Raven, and Starfire."

As technicians wrapped tight ropes around the four Titans, Jade said, "Robin, I want you standing heroically over your trussed-up teammates. You've been injured, but you must go on. Okay, cue the weather! Lights! And...*action*!"

As the actor playing Slade ran from the room, Robin jumped to his feet.

"You won't get away, Slade!" yelled Robin.

"You're hurt, Robin," said Raven as she struggled against the tight ropes around her. She magically grabbed hold of Robin's cape. "You can't go after him," she pleaded.

"Let me go!" protested Robin.

Jade called out from the front of the set, "More frustration, Robin! They're keeping you from your goal! From what you want! Just like they always have!"

Robin tugged on his cape and said, louder, "Let me go! Let me go!"

"More emotion," said Jade. "They've always held you back!"

"Let … me … go!" Robin yelled angrily.

"More! More!" encouraged Jade.

"LET ME GO!" Robin screamed at the top of his lungs.

As the other Titans reacted with shock to Robin's outburst, Jade ran onto the set and hugged him.

"Cut!" she called out. "Robin, one word: *wow.* You're a natural! Great job today! That's how a *real* hero handles his pathetic teammates."

Robin blushed with pleasure and turned to the other Titans. As Jade left the scene, they slowly removed the ropes that had been binding them.

"Did you hear that?" Robin said happily. "Oh, isn't Jade amazing?"

"She is a monster," replied Raven.

"What are you talking about?" Robin said with surprise. "She's making us look like real heroes."

Cyborg shook his head and said, "No, bro. She's making *you* look good. She's making us look like dopes!"

Robin frowned and said, "Well, it's about time people knew the truth. And people are finally going to see me as a real hero!"

He spun around and marched away from the other Titans. A deep growl emerged from Beast Boy.

Raven turned to Beast Boy and said, "Yeah, I feel the same way."

"Nah, that's my tummy, man!" replied Beast Boy. "I'm starving!"

POOF!

Beast Boy transformed himself into a hungry green dog and started sniffing the air in search of food. He trotted to the open door of the sound stage and called out, "This is it, yo!"

The other three Titans ran to the door and saw a large catering table piled high with food and drink.

"Time to get our eat on!" said Cyborg happily.

"Look at all that opulence, yo!" said Beast Boy.

"It is so the fancy, the table has the blanket!" added Starfire.

Beast Boy jumped onto the table, pushing aside a sign that read RESERVED FOR THE JUSTICE LEAGUE. He started grabbing sandwiches.

"Dig in!" he said.

Soon, the four Titans were happily scarfing down food. At first, they didn't even notice Jade Wilson entering the room. She was carrying some blueprints in her hands. Members of the Justice League followed behind her. The heroes were carrying large metal devices in their hands, and they all had dazed looks on their faces.

Seeing Jade and the Justice League enter the room, the Titans quickly jumped underneath the table to hide. They peeked out from below the tablecloth and watched as the Justice League heroes attached their metal devices to a large structure. It looked as if Jade was supervising them while they built some kind of giant machine. After they finished, Jade and the heroes closed a door that hid the machine from view.

Raven turned to her teammates and said, "We gotta get back and tell Robin!"

However, when the Titans found Robin, he was in no mood to listen to his teammates and their talk about Jade Wilson and a mysterious machine.

"Very funny, guys," Robin said. "You promised to take this seriously, you know!"

"Dude, this is for reals, though!" protested Beast Boy. "We saw it with our own eyes!"

"She's working with Slade," said Raven. "And we can prove it! Slade has been busy. There's been a string of crimes across the country. With advanced technology stolen at each location."

"And none of the super heroes were there to stop him!" added Starfire. "Because they were too busy making the movies instead!"

"Slade stole that laser projector from S.T.A.R. Labs," said Beast Boy.

"Combined with all these other things, Slade could build a doomsday device!" warned Cyborg.

"Doomsday device?" replied Robin with scorn. "That's ridiculous! Haven't you guys been paying attention? Everything here's fake! You must have seen a prop. And why would the Justice League help Jade if she was *evil*? That doesn't even make any sense!"

"The Jade has put them under the mind control!" offered Starfire.

"You really think Jade is capable of that?" Robin asked sarcastically.

"Well, she has caused you to act like a different person," said Raven.

Robin stomped his foot on the floor and said, "That's *gratitude* for you! I pulled you guys out of a dumpster; I gave up my own superstardom to focus on the Teen Titans. For once, I've got a chance to get what I want, and you're going to ruin it for me!"

"Yo, you sounds like Robin from the movie," said Beast Boy. "Not the real Robin."

Robin frowned at his teammates and said, "Maybe movie-Robin *is* the real Robin!"

"Well, the real Robin would believe us," replied Raven.

"And, bro, real Robin *trusts* his friends," added Beast Boy.

"And, dude, we're your friends," said Cyborg.

"You must believe the us," said Starfire.

Robin shook his head angrily and sulked. The four other Titans were at a loss for what to do next. Then they saw Jade Wilson moving cautiously on the other side of the sound stage. Superman was floating in the air, following closely behind. Jade stepped into the room containing the giant machine. She shut the door behind her. Superman remained outside the door, standing guard.

Raven whispered to Robin, "See? She's acting really weird."

"We need to get into that room," said Robin with determination.

"But how can we get past the Superman?" asked Starfire.

"We can exploit his number one weakness," suggested Cyborg.

With that, he took out a phone from his mechanical torso. He quickly placed a call to Superman.

RIIIING!

Superman snapped open his phone and said, "Hello?"

Using a high-pitched voice, Cyborg did his best impression of a woman.

"Superman! It's me, your girlfriend! Lois Lane!" he squeaked.

"Well, hello, Lois!" replied Superman. "How are you, my sweet little dewdrop?"

"How am I? I'm terrible!" squealed Cyborg-Lois. "You gotta save me from a nefarious real estate scheme! *Eeek!*"

"Oh my goodness!" said Superman with alarm. "That sounds *terrible*!"

"You'd better hurry, fool," continued Cyborg-Lois. "Or no more smoochie-smoochies!"

"I'm coming, Lois!" Superman cried out, then soared through the air and flew out of the sound stage.

The Teen Titans moved quickly to the door. With trembling hands, Robin cautiously opened the door and led his teammates into the darkened room. His eyes widened in shock as he beheld a giant machine that reached to the ceiling of the sound stage.

"Raven, you were right!" he said. "I've been so blind. We have to destroy this thing before it can do any harm."

Just then, Jade stepped in front of them.

"I see you've found my little secret," she said with a smile.

"You're helping Slade build a doomsday device!" said Cyborg.

"And we're about to take it out, yo!" declared Beast Boy.

Jade shook her head and said, "Whoa, whoa, whoa! I mean, how stupid can you *be*?"

She pointed to the giant machine and said, "This? This right here? This is my O.T.T.V.O.D!"

"Your O.T.T.V. what, now?" asked Robin.

Jade sighed and said, "I didn't want to share this with anyone until it was completed, but here we are."

She continued, "Once finished, the O.T.T.V.O.D will broadcast my movies onto all screens, everywhere in the world. Movie theaters, televisions, phones, tablets, smartwatches, microwaves, you name it. The population of earth will be able to watch super hero movies anywhere, anytime, all the time!"

"Wait, so that's just a big old movie projector?" asked Cyborg.

"So you really are making a Teen Titans movie?" added Robin.

"Of course," replied Jade. "It was going to be the first movie to utilize the O.T.T.V.O.D, in fact."

"Ha! Well, this is just a hilarious misunderstanding," said Cyborg.

"Our bad," added Beast Boy. "This one's on us, yo."

Robin hung his head in shame and said, "Miss Wilson. Jade, I'm so sorry."

"I'm not upset with you, Robin," replied Jade. "You're a star, and you always have been. It's your teammates that I just can't deal with. They've manipulated you into thinking I'm some sort of super-villain. I really hate to do this, but it's over. I'm killing the movie."

The Titans gasped in shock, and Robin hung his head, heartbroken.

"My movie...my dream..." he mumbled.

Cyborg reached out his hand to touch Robin's shoulder and said, "It's all right, bro."

"Yeah, who cares what she thinks, anyway?" added Beast Boy.

Robin spun around and shouted at his teammates, "And it's all your fault!"

"Say what?" asked a surprised Beast Boy.

"I said it's *all your fault*!" Robin raged. "You guys promised to take this seriously! But you couldn't help yourselves, could you?"

"Come on, bro, we didn't—" began Beast Boy.

"This was my chance to *shine*!" said Robin. "And you guys blew it for me!"

"But we—" began Cyborg.

"You ruined everything, just like you always do," Robin said with a sigh. "I guess you really are just a bunch of *jokes*!"

Jade was watching Robin's outburst closely, and she said, "I see your passion, Robin. And I *love* it. What do you say we make a movie about you? And *only you*? Without your stupid friends to mess everything up?"

86

Robin looked at Jade with a smile on his face and said, "A Robin movie? All about me?"

"Phooey, that's ridiculous," observed Cyborg.

"He'd never do us like that, yo!" declared Beast Boy.

"Yeah, out of the question," added Raven.

"Robin made us who we are!" said Starfire. "He would never—"

Before she could finish her sentence, Robin shouted, "I'll do it!"

"What?" asked the stunned Titans.

"A Robin movie," replied Robin. "I'll do it!"

"Bro, is you for reals gonna ditch us?" asked Beast Boy.

"But we have done all of this for you," Starfire said.

"Ha! Done all of what?" said Robin bitterly. "Nearly ruined my movie? We have to face it. *Nothing* ever goes right for us when we're together! It'll be best for everyone if we go our separate ways."

Jade nodded encouragingly and said, "That's a very mature thing to say, Robin. Such bravery."

She faced the other Titans and shouted, "You heard him. You're done! Finished! *Get out!*"

Robin turned away from his teammates and said, "I'm sorry, guys, but this is for the best."

Raven frowned and said, "Fine, go make your own movie. I'm going home to my demon father."

Beast Boy shrugged and said, "Well, the dumpster it is."

"I guess I'll have to be a pro football star after all," said Cyborg.

Starfire sadly moved closer to Robin and reached out her hands to hug her teammate.

"Good luck to you, Robin," she said. "I hope to one day see your movie. I think it will be very good."

Robin gulped and began, "Star, I..."

Before he could finish, Starfire flew away. Robin hung his head and watched as Raven, Cyborg, and Beast Boy walked out of the sound stage.

"Don't worry about them," said Jade, reaching out to touch Robin's shoulder. "Trust me, Robin, you're not alone. You're a big Hollywood star!"

Within seconds, Robin had forgotten about his

teammates. Starfire, Cyborg, Beast Boy, and Raven didn't matter anymore.

He. Was. Ready.

"A *star*!" he said, a dreamy expression on his face. "A big-time Hollywood superstar!"

CHAPTER 7

And so began Robin's new life as an A-list Hollywood celeb-rity. When he stepped onto the red carpet at a movie premiere, he was mobbed by fans who screamed his name and fainted. News reporters crowded near him, shouting out questions.

"Robin, tell us about the movie you're making!" yelled one reporter.

"Robin, do you ever plan on working with the Teen Titans again?" yelled another.

"Well, I—I—" stammered Robin.

"Move along," instructed Jade Wilson, who had stepped up behind Robin. She gave him a gentle shove.

Meanwhile, the other Teen Titans were leading less exciting lives.

Cyborg signed up with professional football team,

but he found that his days were filled with push-ups and sit-ups and collisions with giant football players.

Raven returned to her father's demon dimension and glumly agreed to help Trigon take over Earth.

Starfire reluctantly signed up to fight in a gladiator pit on an alien planet.

And Beast Boy climbed into a dumpster, transformed himself into a goat, and settled down to eat garbage every day. Tears of sadness slowly dripped from his goat eyes as he remembered his happy days as a Teen Titan.

Late one night, Robin sat in a canvas chair in the middle of a sound stage. He scrolled through his communicator, looking at old photos of himself and the other Titans.

"I wonder how they're doing now," he said with a sigh.

Suddenly, Jade popped up behind him.

"They're doing great!" she said.

"They are?" asked Robin.

"Yes! I called them all to see if they wanted to make cameos in the film," Jade said. "But they're all too busy with their fabulous lives away from you."

"Oh, ouch," said Robin. "Well, maybe splitting up was for the best."

"I believe so," said Jade firmly. "Now focus! We're about to film the final scene of your movie!"

"The final scene…" Robin muttered sadly as he walked over to the set of the Titans Tower living room. A replica of the Titans' vault stood in the corner.

"Good," said Jade. "Now, picture this: Slade is finished, and you've returned to the Tower. You open the vault, locking his doomsday device away forever, along with the pain of your past. Then you emerge as a new man. Think you can act that?"

Robin smiled knowingly and said, "Act it? Lady, I've *lived* it!"

Jade smiled back at Robin. "*Annnnnd…*action!" she called out.

Robin stepped toward the vault and stood dramatically in front of the access panel.

KER-BLAM!

Suddenly, a large metal-and-glass light came crashing down from the top of the sound stage. It landed on Robin's head and knocked the young hero facedown onto the floor.

Everything went black. Then Robin heard Jade running toward him to help. He blinked, and the room started coming back into focus.

"Robin? Robin!" she yelled. "Can you hear me?!"

Robin moaned softly and slowly climbed to his feet.

"Wha-what happened?" he asked woozily.

Jade sighed with relief and said, "Oh, thank goodness. A light fell and knocked you out." She held Robin's arm. "Let's wrap for the day so you can recover, and we'll start fresh tomorrow."

"No, I'm fine," said Robin. "Let's finish this movie."

Jade smiled in gratitude and said, "And that's what makes you a *real* hero!"

Robin walked up to the vault again and stared at the access panel. A mechanical voice emerging from the vault said, "Facial scan accepted!"

"Whoa, these effects are pretty impressive!" said Robin. "This is *just* like our vault!"

Jade smiled and said, "Too cool, right? Now please, type in the code."

Robin faced the camera, winked, and wiggled his fingers to push a few random buttons on the access panel.

"Invalid code!" said the vault.

Jade frowned and said, "No, no! It has to feel authentic! Go again!"

Robin pushed the buttons again.

"Invalid code!"

"Come on, Robin," said Jade. "You can do better than that! Stop wasting my time! Again!"

"All right, fine," said Robin. "I'll punch in the real code even though this is just a prop vault."

After pushing the correct buttons, the vault said, "Code accepted. Vault access granted."

SWOOSH!

The vault door sprung open, revealing the telescope lens that Slade had tried to steal from the observatory.

Jade rushed forward and quickly said, "Cut! That was perfect! Brilliant! Robin, thank you! You're a genius."

Robin bowed slightly and tried to appear modest.

"Thank you, thank you," he said. "However, I can do another take if you want me to."

"Nope, that won't be necessary," said Jade as she and Robin walked into the vault.

"Wow, this vault set is really amazing," said Robin. "It looks so real!"

"Because it is real," replied Jade. "We ran into significant budget issues because of your *brilliant* wardrobe—among other, better, more expensive things—so I thought you wouldn't mind shooting at the real Tower! Jade Wilson always finishes her films, no matter what!"

Robin laughed in response, thinking that Jade was joking.

"No, really," Jade continued. "While you were knocked out by our lighting '*accident*,' I moved you to the actual Titans Tower so you could open the vault for me!"

"*Good* one!" said Robin with a chuckle. "That would make a great villain plot."

Jade nodded in agreement and said, "We'll do it in the sequel!"

96

She then peered over Robin's shoulder and pointed.

"What's that behind you?" she said.

Robin turned around to look behind him.

This time, there really was something behind him: Slade, dramatically making his entrance!

Slade clamped metal restraints on Robin's arms, pinning him to the wall of the vault. Jade looked momentarily guilty before grabbing the film from the camera and running out of the room.

"No! Slade, what are you doing?" Robin yelled.

Slade smiled and said, "All of this, the Titans movie, the breakup with your friends, the Robin movie, was all simply..." Slade finished his sentence with two words: *"Mind manipulation!"*

Slade walked over to the lens and grabbed it.

"Ahhh, the final piece of my plan," he said.

He then turned to Robin and said, "Thank you, Robin. You played your role perfectly. You were so desperate to be in a movie, you turned your back on everything important to you. Even your own friends! It was a simple matter of waiting until Jade was desperate and over budget enough on her many super-hero projects for me to swoop in with an offer she couldn't refuse. I would bankroll her films for her help with my plan. She was the perfect Hollywood accomplice!"

"The other super heroes will stop you!" declared Robin.

"A shame they're too busy making movies to stop me," said Slade with a laugh.

Robin struggled to escape from the manacles, but they were too tight.

"This is your final scene, Robin," Slade said as he removed a small bomb detonator device from his pocket. His finger was poised on top of a button on the device.

"And... *action*!" He pushed the button three times. *BOOM! BOOM! BOOM!*

Three giant bombs exploded at the base of Titans Tower. Flames erupted on every floor of the building. Robin watched helplessly as Slade ran from the room.

The fire quickly devoured the Titans' kitchen, living room, and bedrooms. Soon, the flames were marching toward Robin. Thick black smoke filled the vault.

"How could I have been so stupid?" Robin said sadly. "I'm not a real hero, I'm a failure...with no friends...and tiny little baby hands."

Robin sighed and leaned back, waiting for the flames to engulf him.

Just then, he had an idea.

"Baby hands!" he said.

Robin wiggled his fingers and easily slipped his tiny hands out of his gloves. He pulled free of the manacles.

"Ha-ha, yes!" he shouted triumphantly. "Bless you, you stumpy, pudgy little baby hands!"

He kissed his hands in gratitude, but then jumped back as the ceiling started to cave in.

"Uh-oh," he said. "I'd better get out of here."

As flames erupted around him, Robin ran from the room. He made his way down a long, smoke-filled hallway and jumped into a tube that led to a room where the large, metal-encased Titans robot was located. Flames surrounded Robin and the robot.

RUUUUUMBLE!

Suddenly, an entire wall caved in. It buried the robot underneath rubble.

Robin ran to a large window and crashed through it. He then activated a flotation device as he used a glider to soar safely to the small bay of water surrounding the Titans Tower. He swam to the edge of the water and sat down.

WHOMP!

Robin looked up and watched as the Titans Tower started shaking and swaying. Seconds later, the entire building crumbled into the bay. The Tower was destroyed.

Feeling incredibly sad and lonely, Robin reached for his communicator and sent a message to the Teen Titans:

"Titans, it's Robin. I don't know if you'll get this transmission, but I need your help. I know you're all happier in your new lives; I know I said we were holding each other back. But I was wrong. I thought we needed a movie to be real heroes, but we were already real heroes, because we were a team. And I threw that all away. I'm going to Hollywood to set things right.

If I don't make it back, I'm sorry, guys. I never meant to let you down. You all just mean so much to me."

A solitary tear dripped onto Robin's communicator. But the tear hadn't come from him. Suddenly, he heard a voice behind him.

"Excuse me...sorry," said a teary Cyborg. "I get just so emotional when it comes to these type of scenes!"

Robin spun around to see that all the Teen Titans were standing behind him. They were all crying.

"You guys are *back*?" said Robin with delight.

"Of course we're back, fool!" replied Beast Boy. "Do you think I *like* living in a dumpster?"

"It was hard to be without the friends," added Starfire.

Raven pointed toward the middle of the bay and asked, "Uh, Robin? What the heck happened to our Tower?"

Robin smiled sheepishly and said, "Oh yeah. Heh heh heh. The Tower, right. Listen, that's not important now. What's important is that you guys are back! Cyborg! Beast Boy! Starfire! Raven! You're the best super heroes a friend could ask for!"

"Alone, we are the alone," agreed Starfire. "But together, we are..."

"Together!" shouted the Titans.

"Like peanut butter and jelly!" shouted Cyborg. "Like rice and beans!"

"Together!" shouted the Titans.

"We put the *team* in *teen*!" yelled Beast Boy.

"There's no *team* in *teen*," muttered Raven.

"Together!" shouted the Titans.

Robin raised his hand and declared, "We are the Teen Titans. We stand strong, and we stand..."

"Together!" shouted the Titans.

"Okay, gang, back to business," said Robin. "We need to get back to Hollywood. This is going to sound crazy, but Jade Wilson—"

Raven interrupted, "Was actually manipulated by Slade, and the super hero movies are part of his plot to take over the world."

The other Titans looked at her in amazement.

Raven shrugged and said, "Saw it coming a mile away."

"Okay, Titans," said Robin as he ran down the street. "It's time to stop *Slade*!"

CHAPTER 8

Back in Hollywood, spotlights were sweeping through the sky for another movie premiere. This one was being held on the Warner Bros. Studios lot. A large gathering of celebrities had lined up on the red carpet outside the theater. A giant banner proclaimed the first screening of *Robin: The Movie.*

Every super hero who was even remotely super had arrived for the premiere. A movie studio golf cart slowly inched its way toward the theater and stopped at the entrance. Jade Wilson was riding in the cart, and she waved happily to the super heroes as they applauded for her. She stepped out of the cart to address the excited crowd. As an executive at a big-time movie studio, she was used to living by the mantra "the show must go on." She assumed that Slade had lived up to his end of the deal, and she would have another blockbuster on her hands.

"Super ladies and super gentlemen," she called out, "I am thrilled to present my latest film, *Robin: The Movie!*"

The heroes burst into cheers. Jade continued, "And with the help of our new O.T.T.V.O.D technology, the Robin movie will be broadcast simultaneously to every screen on the planet. The entire population of Earth will experience this mind-blowing story at the *same time!*"

Jade pointed toward the famous Warner Bros. water tower in the distance. Next to it was the O.T.T.V.O.D device, a giant, gleaming metal machine.

"Unfortunately," Jade said sadly, "our star, Robin, can't be here tonight because, uh…he has explosive diarrhea. But he insisted that tonight was too important, and the show *must* go on!"

The crowd clapped and cheered, and Jade said, "So without further ado, sit back, relax, and—"

BLAM!

Suddenly, the Teen Titans burst onto the movie lot and marched up to Jade.

"Enjoy us ruining Slade's plan!" Cyborg called out, interrupting Jade.

"Ohhh!" added Beast Boy. "Cyborg finished your sentence, fool!"

Robin faced Jade and said sternly, "This evil plan ends here!"

The super heroes who were gathered on the red carpet gasped in shock.

Superman whispered to Batman, "Wow! Fighting through explosive diarrhea. What a champ!"

Robin turned toward the super heroes.

"I do have something explosive, but it's not diarrhea," he said. "It's the truth! The Robin movie—and, in fact, *all* super hero movies—are actually part of a villainous scheme to take over the world!"

The super heroes gasped again.

Jade looked around nervously.

"How absurd!" she said.

"Oh, is it?" replied Robin. "Then why don't you

tell everyone what could happen if your fancy new technology falls into the wrong hands?"

Robin bounded into the air, did an impressive backflip over Jade's head, and pointed dramatically to the O.T.T.V.O.D in the distance.

As he did, another mysterious figure burst equally dramatically onto the scene to make sure his plan went off without any interruptions.

"Slade!" concluded Robin.

The super heroes gasped yet again. Jade ran away.

"The machine he built isn't for sharing movies," said Raven. "It's some sort of doomsday weapon! He used Jade!"

"Game over, Slade," said Robin smugly. "You've got to deal with us and every super hero in the world."

Slade laughed diabolically.

"I'm sorry, Robin," he said. "But the heroes work for *me* now!"

Slade pushed a button on his wrist and activated the O.T.T.V.O.D device. Instantly, all the heroes on the red carpet went into a trance.

"Titans! Look away!" Robin called out.

With a dazed look on his face, Superman and the other super heroes stared at the Teen Titans. Their minds were being controlled by Slade.

"Oh, hey," said Superman slowly. "Is that the Robin movie?"

"Mind control!" said Slade with an evil laugh. "Heroes, step forward!"

The audience of super heroes started moving menacingly toward the Teen Titans.

"We obey," the super heroes intoned. "We obey."

As the super heroes circled the Titans, Slade threw his hands up in the air triumphantly.

"I've taken my mind manipulation to the next level," he called out. "I now have *full* mind control! And as soon as the O.T.T.V.O.D is fully powered, the whole world will be under my mind control!"

Slade pressed the button on his wrist again. The O.T.T.V.O.D began to vibrate.

A mechanical voice emerged from the machine: "Robin movie transmission beginning."

Just then, the machine sent a digital signal into space. That signal bounced off of satellites orbiting

Earth, and soon the signal surrounded the globe. *Robin: The Movie* started to play on movie screens, television screens, and phone screens. Everywhere in the world, people were watching the Robin movie.

But Slade had installed a spinning, hypnotic image on top of the movie. People around the world fell into a deep trance as they stared at their screens.

Back at the studio, the mind-controlled super heroes had surrounded the Teen Titans.

"*Kill* them!" commanded Slade.

"We obey, we obey..." chanted the super heroes.

Beast Boy turned to his teammates and said, "This looks bad, yo."

Just then, Robin noticed the golf cart that had transported Jade to the movie theater.

"Titans, *GO!*" he yelled, and he and his teammates piled into the cart.

"We have to destroy that doomsday device!" Robin said, driving the cart away from the theater.

BLAM!

Robin spun the steering wheel. The cart crashed into a sound stage and bounced off a streetlamp.

"Robin, look out!" yelled Cyborg.

"I think we lost 'em!" Robin said with a smile.

VROOOOM!

Suddenly, the Batmobile zoomed into view and started chasing the Titans.

"There is no stopping the Batman," observed Starfire.

The golf cart made a sharp left turn and careened through the studio. It was headed straight toward the Atom. The pint-size hero was standing in the middle of the road.

"Halt for the mighty Ato—" he began.

SQUISH!

The Atom smashed into the golf cart's windshield.

Raven looked behind her and saw that the other super heroes were gaining on them.

"We can't shake 'em!" she said.

"You keep the super heroes distracted," said Robin. "I'm going after that doomsday device!"

Robin fired a line from his grappling gun and soared through the air. He landed on top of the Warner Bros. water tower. Slade was perched on top of the O.T.T.V.O.D device.

Robin reached into his Utility Belt and removed a grenade. He pulled the pin and tossed it toward the machine. Slade deftly caught the grenade and lobbed it away.

KA-BOOM!

Sound stage 4 was blown into bits.

"It's time to finish this, Slade," declared Robin.

The villain and the young hero glared at each other high above the movie studio.

Down below, the other Titans had driven to a dead end. The hypnotized super heroes were marching closer and closer.

"How are we supposed to defeat the World's Greatest Super Heroes?" asked Cyborg nervously.

"Portal?" suggested Raven.

"Oh yeah," said Beast Boy.

"We always forget about those," added Cyborg.

POOF!

Raven opened a magical portal that quickly swallowed the crowd of super heroes.

High above the studio, Robin and Slade were now battling atop the O.T.T.V.O.D. Just as Robin was about to throw another explosive device at the machine, the villain held up his hand.

"Are you *sure* you don't want to watch your movie?" he said, pointing to a small screen on the O.T.T.V.O.D. "This is the best part! You *gotta* see this!"

"Nice try, Slade," replied Robin.

"Some people say the camera adds five pounds, but in your case it's, like, five pounds of muscle."

Robin blushed with pride and said, "Well, I *have* been working on my arms...." Then he quickly shook his head and said, "No! Not this time, Slade!"

"But this is your dream, Robin," said Slade. "The world is *finally* seeing you as a real hero. Don't you want to take a peek?"

Robin closed his eyes, but soon he couldn't help but open one eye a bit. Out of the corner of his eye, he watched the flickering images on the screen. He opened both eyes and stared at the screen. He was instantly hypnotized.

"It's…everything…I…ever…wanted," he said in a slow, dreamy voice.

Just then, the other Titans climbed up on top of the O.T.T.V.O.D to join Robin and Slade.

"Robin is under Slade's mind control!" Raven called out.

"Snap out of it, man!" commanded Cyborg.

"You should watch it," muttered Robin in a dull, monotone voice. "It's not bad."

"We can't do that, bro!" said Beast Boy.

Slade glared at the other Titans and said, "They don't like your movie, Robin. Kill them!"

Robin moved toward his teammates. In his hand he held the explosive device.

"Wait, please!" said Starfire. "There is another Robin movie you must see."

"The original!" said Cyborg as he extracted a portable VHS tape player from his mechanical body. He pushed a button and a video started playing. It was the Robin movie that the Teen Titans had created to cheer Robin up.

"Robin was just a little baby boy that lived at the circus. Doin' acrobatics and things," said the announcer in the video.

Robin blinked and seemed momentarily confused.

"But you always thought I was a joke," he said to his teammates.

The announcer's voice continued, "But then he grew up, and he wasn't a baby no more! But he still had them baby hands, yo."

As Robin watched the video, Slade's mind control power began to fade away.

"Robin, you were never a joke to us," said Raven.

"You are our leader," added Starfire.

"Our hero," said Beast Boy.

"Our friend," declared Cyborg.

Robin shook his head, blinked, and smiled at his teammates.

"Titans," he said, "let's take down Slade. *Together!*"

The heroes spun around to confront the villain. But he had escaped.

"Where is he?" wondered Raven.

Beast Boy pointed up to the top of the water tower.

"He's up there, yo!" said Beast Boy.

"I'm always one step ahead, you pathetic goof-sters!" taunted Slade.

Robin called out to Slade, "The world may look at us like goofs that crack jokes and sing songs. But you know what? We're the *Teen Titans*!"

"Our jokes are the strongest," declared Cyborg.

"Our goofs are the goofiest," said Starfire.

"And our songs are the dopest!" added Beast Boy.

"Word," concluded Raven.

"So, you're going to stop me with a song?" Slade sneered.

Robin turned to his teammates and said, "That's *exactly* what we're going to do!"

Before the Titans could launch into their song, though, Slade pressed another button on his wrist. The Warner Bros. water tower began to transform into a giant, multiarmed robot. A chute suddenly extended from it; Slade disappeared into the chute and reappeared within the head of the robot.

WHOMP!

Slade's robot shot out a wave of flames that headed directly toward the Teen Titans.

Thinking quickly, Cyborg pressed a button on his arm and instantly encased the Titans within a metal sphere that repelled the flames.

"Cyborg, call it in!" ordered Robin.

The metal sphere began to beep. It was acting as a beacon to the Titans robot that was buried in the rubble where Titans Tower had stood.

"Come on...come on..." pleaded Cyborg.

Back in Jump City, deep within the pile of Titans Tower debris, the broken mechanical pieces of the Titans robot started to reassemble.

WHOOSH!

The Titans robot was whole again! It zoomed through the air, headed to Hollywood. Minutes later, it arrived outside the sphere where the Teen Titans were huddled together.

"Teen Titans, *GO!*" Robin called out.

Cyborg dismantled the metal sphere and the five heroes hopped inside the Titans robot, where each one took up a battle station.

The Titans robot soared toward Slade's water-tower robot. Both robots swung their mighty arms and crashed into each other. Slade's robot then produced two giant swords and plunged them into the Titans robot.

"Let's finish this on foot with a song," yelled Robin. He and his teammates hopped out of their robot and landed on the ground. "Titans, *GO!*"

With that, Cyborg brought out his trusty cassette, and the group launched into their awesome theme song.

The heroes battled Slade's robot as they sang. They fought bravely. They jumped through the air, trying to avoid the robot's powerful arms.

BLAM! BLAM! BLAM! BLAM! BLAM!

The giant mechanical fists on Slade's robot crashed against the Teen Titans, knocking each hero to the ground.

Just then, a hatch on Slade's robot popped open. The villain emerged to glare at the Titans.

"Any last words, Robin?"

"You...you've got something on your shirt," replied Robin.

Slade looked down at his shirt and said, "I do?"

As Slade studied his shirt, Robin tossed an explosive device onto the villain's chest. The device knocked Slade off balance, and he tumbled off the robot.

KER-BLAM!

The bomb detonated as Slade fell through the air.

WHOMP!

Only Slade's mask landed on the ground. The rest of the villain was nowhere to be seen.

As the smoke from the explosion cleared, Cyborg, Raven, Starfire, and Beast Boy stared at Robin.

"You did it, dude!" said Cyborg proudly.

"You saved the world," added Starfire.

"No, *we* did," said Robin.

Just then, the world's other super heroes emerged from the portal that Raven had created for them. They were no longer under Slade's mind control, and now they gathered around the Titans. They all stared at Robin.

Batman slowly started clapping his gloved hands together. Soon, all the other heroes had joined in the applause.

Robin held up his hands to quiet the crowd. He then cleared his throat and spoke.

"Fellow heroes, we can all agree that movies are

the most important thing in the world," he said. "But we are defenders of the innocent. It is our job to save the world, and *nothing* should ever distract us from that sacred duty! So, I propose, that from this day forward, there will be no more super hero movies *ever again*!"

"*Booooooooo!*"

The heroes angrily rejected Robin's idea.

Cyborg leaned close to Robin and whispered, "Too far, dude!"

Robin turned back to the crowd and quickly said, "Right, okay. Uh, so, what I meant to say is, from this day forward, super heroes will only be played by actors!"

"*Yaaaaay!*"

The heroes now cheered Robin's idea.

One week later, the Titans were gathered within the rubble that had once been the mighty Titans Tower. The heroes were sitting on a half-destroyed couch, and they were watching a broken TV set.

Raven looked around and said, "You know, maybe we should rebuild this place."

Beast Boy emerged from the pile of rubble that had once been their bathroom.

"Why?" he replied. "The plumbing still works!"

Beast Boy and Cyborg high-fived each other and shouted, "*That's* what's up!"

And so, with all potential pooping problems resolved, the Teen Titans resumed their awesome lives.